D0461613

To my mother
—H.H.

Little, Brown and Company • Hachette Book Group USA • 237 Park Avenue, New York, NY 10017 • Visit our Web site at www.lb-kids.com
First Edition: September 2008

Library of Congress Cataloging-in-Publication Data

Hobbie, Holly.
Fanny / by Holly Hobbie.—1st ed.
p. cm.
Summary: Fanny asks for a Connie doll like those of her friends, and when her mother says no, Fanny tries to make one for herself.
ISBN 978-0-316-16687-4
[1. Dolls--Fiction. 2. Dollmaking--Fiction.] I. Title.
PZ7.H6517Fan 2008
[E]--dc22
2007048376

10 9 8 7 6 5 4 3 2 1
TWP
Printed in Singapore
The paintings for this book were done in watercolor. • The text was set in Cantoria MT.

Fanny

Holly Hobbie

LB 1837

LITTLE, BROWN AND COMPANY
New York Boston

For her birthday this year, Fanny had her heart set on a Connie doll. She had asked for a Connie for her last birthday, and then again for Christmas, too. It was the only kind of doll she wanted.

But Fanny's mother was very clear. "I'm not going to get you one of those Connie dolls, so please stop asking for one."

"MOM," Fanny said, "everybody has one."

That was true. Fanny's two best friends both had Connie dolls, which they adored.

"The answer is no," her mother said.

"Why?"

"Because I don't like the way Connie dolls look," said her mother. "They're just too . . . much."

Fanny was in such a fluster she thought she'd POP.
Then she had an idea.

"All right," she said to herself, "I'll just make my own Connie."

She cut out pieces of a pink pajama top and sewed them into arms and legs and a longish body. She stuffed all the different parts with cotton and sewed them together. She drew a very cheerful face on the head and for hair she used a bunch of bright yarn.

Fanny worked on her doll all afternoon and at last she was done.
"There's my Connie," she said decidedly.

The doll just smiled.

"Hmm," Fanny reconsidered, looking harder at the doll's face in the mirror. "Maybe Connie isn't exactly the best name for you." Then it came to her. "How about...Annabelle?" she said.

And Fanny clearly heard a little voice pipe up. The doll seemed to say, "I like that name. Call me Annabelle."

When Fanny's mother peeked into the room, she burst into a big smile. "What a wonderful doll."

"Do you really think so?" Fanny asked. "She's not funny looking?"

"I think she's marvelous," her mother said.

That night Fanny tucked Annabelle into bed and gazed at her for a long time. "I made you," she said. "I can hardly believe it. Maybe you *are* marvelous."

The next day, Fanny invited her two best friends to come over for her birthday, and they both brought along their Connies. Soon they were busy dressing them and combing their long hair and posing them as gorgeous models and sassy celebrities.

Before long, Fanny brought out her homemade doll.
"Guess what," she said proudly. "This is Annabelle."
Her friends didn't say a word.

Fanny tried to include Annabelle in the activities, but her friends acted like Annabelle wasn't even there. She *did* look sort of puffed up and odd compared to the Connies, Fanny had to admit. Finally, she took the doll into her bedroom and stuffed her into a dresser drawer.

"Come on, girls," Fanny's mother called. "Time for cake and presents."

Fanny's biggest present was a real sewing machine along with a bundle of fabric, a box of assorted buttons, ribbons, and bright balls of yarn.

"Thanks, Mom," she smiled. But deep down, she didn't feel like ever making anything again.

"I'm glad I never got a present like that," Tiffany said, laughing. "I can't even sew."

"I like store-bought anyway," said Coco. "It looks more professional."

BEGINNER'S
Sewing
Machine

That night Fanny couldn't fall asleep because she couldn't stop thinking about Annabelle. Maybe she was afraid of the dark, Fanny thought. Of course, that was impossible because she was just a doll, after all. Or maybe she was lonely. That seemed impossible, too, but what if she was?

Fanny went to the dresser and pulled open the drawer.
There was Annabelle smiling up at her.

Fanny frowned. "I must admit, you *are* different."

Then she heard that little voice again. The doll seemed to say,
"You made me. Don't you love me?"

Fanny lifted Annabelle into her arms. "Of course I do," she said. She felt herself brighten with a warm glow. "And I think you're beautiful."

She carefully settled Annabelle into bed and snuggled close beside her.

"And you are so soft and cuddly, too," Fanny said. "Goodnight, Annabelle. Sleep tight. Tomorrow is going to be a busy day."

The following morning, Tiffany called to invite Fanny over to her house. Coco would be there as well. With her dolls, of course.

"I'll ask Annabelle if she wants to come," Fanny said.

"You can play with our Connies," Tiffany offered. "We have extras."

"But I think Annabelle wants to come," Fanny told her. "I'm almost positive."

At Tiffany's, Fanny thought it was a perfect day to play veterinary hospital, and her friends agreed.

"The Connie dolls can be nurses," they cried, clapping their hands.

"And I think I know of a wonderful doctor," said Fanny.

All afternoon, Dr. Annabelle performed operations on every stuffed animal Tiffany owned—emergency after emergency—while the glamorous nurses assisted.

That evening, Fanny's mother looked into her bedroom.

"What are you up to in here?" she asked. "You've been so busy."

"I'm making some clothes for Annabelle," Fanny said. "She only had one dress to wear."

After she made Annabelle two new jumpers, she thought of something else every little girl needed, and she made that, too, one step at a time.

"This is your very own doll," Fanny said. "What shall we name her?"

Annabelle was smiling. "We could call her Dolly," she said.

"That's too ordinary," Fanny replied. "How about . . . Sally?"

And now Fanny heard a new, tiny voice pipe up.

"I don't think I like that name," said Annabelle's doll.

"Well, what name would you like?" Fanny asked, surprised.

"Connie," said the new little doll. "Call me Connie."

"Hmm," Fanny considered. "I'm sure there's never been a Connie like you."

"Yes," said Annabelle positively. "Let's call you Connie."

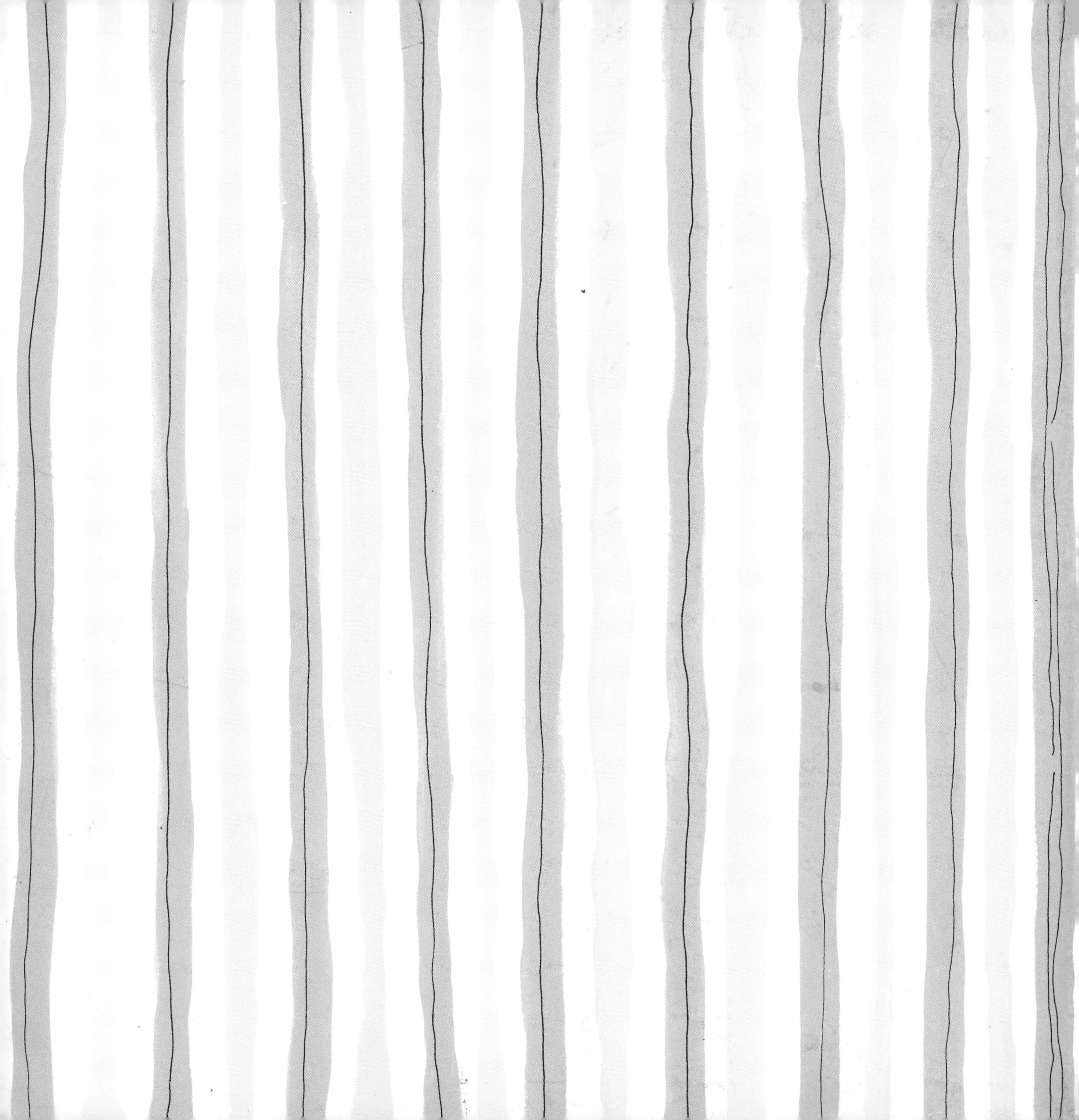